flashed the screen.

Think carefully? I had done with thinking carefully. I had to get the photograph. I had to get the vase. I had to spin through time to 1990. And while I was there, I would skateboard and swim; I would race an Elizabethan bicycle down a steep hill; I would use my nose to smell things and I would taste fishes' fingers. Just like Gran had said.

I was shivering from head to foot. I wasn't sure whether it was from excitement. Or from fear.

I was going to be a Time Spinner.

TIME SPINNER

ROY APPS

Illustrated by Susan Varley

RED FOX

A Red Fox Book
Published by Random House Children's Books
20 Vauxhall Bridge Road, London SW1V 2SA

A division of Random House UK Ltd

London Melbourne Sydney Auckland
Johannesburg and agencies throughout the world

First published in 1990 by Andersen Press Ltd

Red Fox edition 1992

5 7 9 10 8 6 4

Text © 1990 by Roy Apps
Illustrations © 1990 by Andersen Press Ltd

Printed and bound in Great Britain by
Cox & Wyman Ltd, Reading, Berkshire

RANDOM HOUSE UK Limited Reg. No. 954009

Papers used by Random House UK Limited
are natural, recyclable products made from wood grown in
sustainable forests. The manufacturing processes conform to
the environmental regulations of the country of origin

ISBN 0 09 981800 0

Contents

Contents

1
Imagining

It all started with the fishes' fingers.

I was alone in my BedCube. Lying on the bed with my eyes shut. Imagining I was alive in Elizabethan times; back in the 1990s. Bicycle-riding, skateboarding, swimming—it must have been great to have been an Elizabethan.

'Rosemary!' Mum's voice boomed from the corridor. 'We're off now!'

I don't know why she sounded so excited. Dad was

only taking her to the Wilkinses at number 4023 for a SupaDisk SoftWare Party. Yawn. Bore. All they do at these SoftWare parties is to sit around and swap one old DigiTuneDisk for another even older Digi-TuneDisk. They all sound the same anyway. Yawn. Bore.

I carried on imagining. This is what I imagined. I was bent over the steering handle of a bright red Elizabethan bicycle, racing hard down a steep, steep hill. Trees and buildings flashed past me in a whirl of colour and the wind whined and whistled through my ears.

'Have you gone deaf or something?' Mum was standing over me. Hands on hips.

'Eh?'

'I've been calling you for the last five minutes.'

Now Dad was on the scene.

'She spends too much time lying around moping, if you ask me,' he said.

I *didn't* ask you, I thought.

'I don't mope,' I said.

'Well, I don't know what else you'd call it.'

I don't suppose you would, I thought.

'Imagining,' I said.

'Imagining has no useful function for anyone. You're old enough to know that by now.'

Why does everything have to be *useful?* I thought.

'We won't be late back, love.' Mum's turn.

'Oh . . . ?'

She gave me one of her quizzical looks. Did I sound too disappointed? Did she suspect what I had in mind?

'What homework have you got tonight?'

'Elementary Astronomy and Technology.'

'Now, you *will* finish it before going to bed?'

'Of course, Mum.' My eyes smiled sweetly, but my fingers were tightly crossed behind my back; something Gran had taught me to do.

Elementary Astronomy and Technology are the last things you would *choose* to do if you were alone in the Domestic Living Unit with Gran. Because those times are brilliant times. Listening to Gran talk about the olden days is like having a busy picture painted for you in front of your very eyes. It's the only thing in the whole of the wide universe that's better than imagining.

'Bye!'

I lay back on my bed and looked around. Welcome to my BedCube. Yawn. Bore. A curved white ceiling reflects a pool of gentle light all round. All the furniture is moulded in pastel laminates: a pale pink dressing-table, soft green bed and chairs, grey VDU, grey TeleSatScreen. Yawn. Bore.

'What are you complaining about?' That's what Dad always says: 'It's clean and it's spacious and it's warm and it's comfortable . . . .'

And it's just like *their* BedCube.

And it's just like Gran's BedCube.

It's just like every other cube in our Domestic Living Unit and every other Domestic Living Unit on the European Space Colony (Taurus IV).

And probably just like every Domestic Living Unit on Aquarius and Pisces, too. Not that I've never been there.

I heard the hiss of the Domestic Living Unit door closing as Mum and Dad left for the Wilkinses. I listened, then counted to five; listened again. All was quiet. I sat up, swung my legs round and leapt off the bed.

I pushed the bright green button by my BedCube door. It swished open. It always does. Yawn. Bore. Nothing ever breaks down on the European Space Colony (Taurus IV). I padded across the walkway and pushed the bright green button outside Gran's BedCube door.

2
Relics

It swished open. Of course.

'Gran? Are you asleep?'

She usually has a nap in the evenings.

'Yes. Out for the count. Snore, snore.'

'Eh? Oh Gran . . . .'

'Well, come on in if you're going to, you great
wally.'

Gran's BedCube is well, exactly like my BedCube;
except for our secret. Which is a box of ancient relics
under the bed. On very special occasions and only
when Mum and Dad are out we open the box up and
look at and touch the relics. Ancient relics are strictly
forbidden in Domestic Living Units on the European
Space Colony Taurus IV. Which makes Gran a
criminal. And probably me, too.

'What's a great wally, Gran?'

'Eh? Oh, I don't know. It's an old-fashioned
phrase. Something my mum often used to call my
dad.'

'Yes, but what does it *mean?*'

'Well . . . I suppose . . . twit.'

'Eh?'

'Well, what does your mum call you when you've

been a bit silly?'

'A proper dilt.'

'There you are then. Great wally is just an old-fashioned phrase meaning a proper dilt. Now, what do you want for supper?'

Supper. Yawn. Bore.

I went to Gran's dressing-table and entered the code on her VDU—RO:JE:MA. I like my code RO:JE:MA. I often say it in my head as one word: Rojema. Sometimes in my imaginings, I call myself Rojema, rather than Rosemary. The screen flashed up:

RO:JE:MA ROSEMARY JEMIMA MARTIN
(PROGRAM: BODICARE)
ID No: WD/YT/80/B67210
Domestic Living Unit 4057
The European Space Colony (Taurus IV)

DATELINE: 2:10:2090

Hi Rosemary! For supper tonight, Rosemary, you need:

D2 6ml B1 2ml C 30ml

Bon appetit!

If that was what the Bodicare Program said I wanted for supper, that was what I'd got to have for supper. Three tablets popped out of the dispenser and I swallowed them all in one giant gulp.

'Gran, did the Elizabethans have tablets for supper?'

'Of course not.'

'What did they have then?'

Gran looked around and listened intently. She leaned over towards me.

'Promise you'll tell no one I told you.'

'Promise.'

'Cross your heart; hope to die?'

'Cross my heart; hope to die, Gran.'

That was another Elizabethan phrase Gran had taught me. She put her head close to mine; I could hear her breathing very quickly.

'Dead plants and animals.'

My stomach suddenly felt as if it was being pulled up towards my throat.

'Dead plants and animals?'

Gran nodded. Her face was as steady as a rock.

'And they had a special delicacy . . . .'

If dead plants and animals were the Elizabethans' usual diet, I wasn't sure I wanted to hear about their special delicacies. But already Gran was whispering in my ear:

'Fishes' fingers.'

My stomach was creeping up the back of my tongue. This had to be one of Gran's famous wind-ups.

'Fishes didn't have fingers. I know; I've seen graphics of them on the History disk.'

'Huh, History disk; mystery disk,' muttered Gran, darkly. 'Of course the graphics you saw of fishes on the History disk didn't have any fingers and do you know why?'

I shook my head.

'The Elizabethans had eaten them all for their supper.'

'Urgh. But why did the Elizabethans eat fishes' fingers?'

Gran shrugged. 'The taste I suppose.'

'Taste?'

'Yes . . . taste. Flavour. A sense they used to have.'

'What was it like?'

'Like? Oh . . . I can't describe it. Any more than you can describe shades and colours. I mean, can you describe "pink" to me?'

'Pink? Well, it's sort of . . . light red.'

'Sort of light red! What's that meant to tell me? I suppose if I asked you to describe "red", you'd say it was sort of dark pink?'

'Er . . . .'

I took Gran's point.

'There you are then. No one can describe colour or taste. Smell—that was another one.'

'Smell?'

'You used your nose for smelling.'

It sounded horrid.

'I remember your great-grandfather lighting a fire. Made from wood. In the open air. That was some smell. Wood smoke.'

Gran's eyes had glazed over. She seemed to be looking somewhere way out beyond the dreamy-white ceiling of the BedCube.

'I miss those tastes and smells,' she said, quietly.

Then she got down onto her knees and crawled under the bed. I held my breath and my heart beat faster. She was dragging out the wooden box of ancient relics.

'Fishes' fingers,' she murmured.

She prised off the lid. She took out a long thin tube of wood with holes in it. This was what the Elizabethans made music on before DigiTune. Then she took out a badge and a tiny plastic model of an Elizabethan petrol-driven car. Then she handed me a large vase made of what she called glass, that shone all the colours of the spectrum. I had seen it everytime Gran had opened her relic box and everytime it seemed more and more magical.

'Careful with that. It's very fragile.'

I tightened my grip on the priceless relic.

'It's beautiful . . . it's fants!' I whispered.

'What the Elizabethans would have called wicked,' said Gran.

I frowned. 'Wicked? But wicked means bad.'

'Yes, I, know. But the Elizabethans used it to mean good, too. Like "That's a really wicked jacket. Or that's a really wicked vase."'

'Wicked meant fants?' I shook my head. There was a lot I didn't understand about the Elizabethans.

Gran was foraging deep into the relic box.

'Ah-ha. That's what they would have eaten them with—a knife and fork.'

She looked up from the box with a big grin and held up a pair of hand-sized, deadly-looking weapons; one with a gleaming blade, the other with

four pointed prongs. I shivered. They sparkled in the light and seemed sharp enough to slice through your tongue.

'Mmm, there might be a picture of a fish's finger in this book,' she muttered.

Even the box itself was something of a relic. I picked it up.

'Gran . . . why does the relic box have such a thick bottom?'

'Rosemary, why are you always asking questions?'

'No! Look inside. The bottom comes a long way up the sides.'

Gran tapped the bottom of the box with her knuckle. It sounded as hollow as a drum.

'Looks to me like a false bottom. Give me that knife.'

Gran eased the knife between the bottom and the inside wall of the box. There was a creaking sound as the false bottom slowly began to lift. When there was a big enough space for her fingers, Gran put her hand in and pulled. The false bottom came completely out.

'Flipping heck,' said Gran. 'Look at that!'

'What is it?'

'It's a photograph.'

'Eh?'

'A photograph—a sort of primitive method of recording two-dimensional graphic images before holographs and spectrographs and the like.'

In this photograph, there was a row of Elizabethan boys and a row of Elizabethan girls. At the bottom it said: 'Turnbury Girls' Football Team. Turnbury Boys' Football Team: Thursday 29th March 1990.'

'Oh my goodness! This is special!' Gran was really excited now. 'Look at that girl in the middle of the back row; who does she remind you of?'

This sounded to me like one of Gran's famous-people-in-Elizabethan-history questions.

'What—the ginger one with the sticking-out ears?'

'Yes . . . .'

I thought hard. Trying desperately to remember the names of all those Elizabethan princesses.

'Princess . . . Someone . . . ?'

'Princess, my foot. It's the spitting image of you, Rosemary.'

'Oh.'

'Yes, this must be a photograph of your great-gran.'

'Which one?'

'Your Great-Gran Samantha. My mother. When she was about your age. She was football crazy.'

I shivered. 'What, do you mean that playing football games made her mad?'

'No I do not!'

Gran told me all about the Elizabethans and their football games. How it was fun, but of no use, just like my imaginings. And all about mud, caused by

rain, which the Elizabethans had no way of controlling. I ran my hand over the photograph; it was smooth, as if it had not been touched for years. I stared hard at the serious, squinting faces and imagined the sound of their giggling and chatter. Everything about the photograph seemed just like a magical dream.

'. . . Your great-gran was the best footballer of them all, you know,' Gran explained.

'Better than the boys?'

'Oh certainly better than any of the boys.' She was staring hard at the faces in the photograph of the boys' football team.

'Is any of those boys my great-grandad then, Gran?' I asked.

And that is why I didn't hear the hiss of the Domestic Living Unit door.

For before Gran could answer, Dad's voice screamed in my ear. 'Rosemary! Back to your own BedCube! This minute!'

I jumped. My hands jarred. As if in slow motion, the priceless glass vase slipped through my fingers, crashed to the floor and with a single thud shattered into hundreds of tiny fragments.

3
Sulk

It was the shock, I suppose, of hearing Dad's voice behind me and the heart-leap as I felt the vase slipping through my fingers. That and the piercing anger gnawing away inside me when I saw the dull pieces of glass lying at my feet. That was what made me turn round and scream at him:

'You stupid, stupid person! You stupid, stupid dilt!'

'Get to your room this instant!' Dad fumed.

'No I won't. You bully. You fat, fat bully blubber!'

Silly words. Words that didn't make much sense. Words I knew deep down that I didn't really mean. It was just . . . being made to jump like that; and dropping the vase.

'Go to your BedCube, Rosemary.' Mum's voice was calm, unflustered. Typical.

I went. Without a word to anyone, I left Gran's cube. I didn't dare glance at Gran, afraid of what I might see written in her face.

I lay face down on my bed and cried hard into the pillow until my whole body shook. I knew Mum would come in to see me soon, and when she did she would see just how angry and upset I was.

But by the time she came in, I'd stopped shaking. I

22

felt flushed and somehow all sort of sad and warm inside. I knew what she was going to say.

'Rosemary . . . . '

'Yes, Mum . . . . '

'Rosemary what have we always told you about relics?'

'Don't touch them.' I sniffed, quietly, in a sad sort of voice.

'And . . . ?'

'And if you see any, contact the Colony Police,' I added. And sniffed again.

'Exactly. And you know perfectly well why . . . . '

'Because they're dangerous,' I sighed.

'Very dangerous. Relics are dirty. Heaven knows what kinds of germs and bacteria they might be carrying, particularly Elizabethan relics. The Elizabethans were a filthy lot.'

'Yes, Mum.'

'That's why the law's so strict. It is to protect us.'

I wanted to say they don't seem to have done Gran any harm. But I dared not.

Mum paused; waiting for me to say something. Silence.

'We could all have been in serious trouble if anyone else had found out about it, Rosemary. You know that.'

Shrug.

Mum came and sat herself down by me on my bed.

'So why do you do it?'

Shrug.

'Mmm?' Mum in her most understanding voice.

Shrug.

'I mean, I can understand Granny going on about the past—she's getting very old now and hasn't much to look forward to—but for a girl your age, Rosemary . . . and apart from the Police, well, I don't think it's very healthy and I don't just mean the germs—I mean for your mind . . . .'

'My mind . . . ?'

'Yes. Moping around, dreaming about the past all the time. It's morbid.'

Perhaps, I thought, perhaps it isn't germs they

were trying to protect us from. Perhaps it was something else. Something less easy to understand than germs. Something I couldn't put a name or a notion to.

'Anyway, there's no need to worry about it any more,' Mum was saying.

'I'm *not* worried. It's you and Dad who are worrying.'

Mum gave one of her big sighs.

'What I mean, Rosemary, is that we will call the matter closed. All right?'

'How can it be closed? What about Gran's relics?'

'Your father's put them all down the MultiFlush.'

I suddenly felt all knotted up inside.

'Down the MultiFlush? But what did Gran say?'

'It's what the law says that matters.'

'But they were *Gran's* relics.'

'They were Gran's junk.'

Every one of Gran's relics churned up, shredded and destroyed by the scorching chemicals and grinding blades of our Domestic Living Unit's MultiFlush. The long thin tube of wood with holes in it; the badge; the tiny plastic model of an Elizabethan petrol-driven car. And the hundreds of pieces of glass vase that had shone all the colours of the spectrum.

And the photograph. With ginger-haired, sticking-out-ears Great-Gran Samantha in the back row of the 1990 Turnbury Girls' football team. The best footballer of them all.

Mum went to the door of my BedCube, then on her way out turned to me.

'And get that homework done before you go to bed.'

She smiled and gave me one of her infuriating looks.

'And do stop that pouting, Rosemary. It's not the end of the world.'

That's what she thought. The end of Gran's relics *was* the end of my world, well, a part of my world, at any rate. My times alone with Gran would never be the same again—she might not ever want to talk to me again, after having broken her glass vase. I hated Dad for being so angry. I hated Mum for being so calm. I hated the world we lived in for having no relics. And I hated myself for destroying the most magical thing that I had ever seen or would be likely to see, ever again.

These were the kind of times when I wished I had a sister to moan and bitch to. Even a brother to shout at would have been something. But I didn't have a sister or a brother. My last friend on Taurus had been Clarissa Morgan-Hicks, but she had moved with her parents out to Colony Aquarius. That's the trouble with space colonies. People move around so much. As soon as you get to know someone, their mum and dad move to a new job out on Pisces or Aquarius.

So I carried on pouting.

Those funny, beautiful, gaudy, heavy old things in the relic box were all gone. And they had belonged to Gran and it was all my fault she had lost them because I had *willed* her to show them to me. And there was no way I could replace them. No way at all.

How could I ever face Gran again?

I lay down on my bed. The curved white ceiling became grey and fuzzy. I closed my eyes and fell asleep.

4
Homework

Nobody spoke at breakfast. The only sounds were the pop-popping of tablets from the Bodicare Program dispenser and Dad yawning.

Every day was like this. Mum and Dad would go off in the SpaceCruiser. Once through the pressure chamber, they would slowly circle the silent, floating mass of plastics and metals known as the European Space Colony (Taurus IV). They worked as general maintenance engineers, checking various components, instruments and installations.

Gran would sit in her room, plug in the DigiTune and view the same dreary holographs. Yawn. Bore.

And I would sit at the keyboard and work at my EduCom. Lessons, lessons, lessons. Every day. Yawn. Bore.

I went across the walkway to the workstation and booted up my computer. Last night's homework appeared on the screen. The question was:

'If the current state of Ante-Temporal Technology allows for a time-slip of 0.3 over 24 for every 50 years covered, what would the time-slip be for a ten—hour voyage covering 25 years? Please use your calculator.'

I stared at the screen. And I thought of Gran's relics. I stared at the calculator. And I thought of Gran. Each time I glanced at the screen all I could see was the photograph.

It was no good. I had to see her. Even if she was into her holograph. Even though I didn't know what I was going to say.

The holograph Gran was viewing was of a deserted Earth beach, with sunshine and sea and sand and trees. She had her DigiTune plug in her ears, so I had to tap her on the shoulder, which made her jump.

'Eh! Oooh! Oh, hello Rosemary.'

'Gran . . . .'

'What is it, love?'

'Gran . . . .'

'If it's last night you're worried about don't.'

'But the vase—'

'It was only an old crock. Just an old woman's silly fancy.'

I didn't believe her.

'I wish I could get you another one.'

'It's no use crying over spilt milk.'

'I'm not crying, Gran.'

She looked hard at me. 'Your mum told me this morning that it had to stop, otherwise we'll all be in trouble with the authorities.'

'What's got to stop?'

'All this talk about the past.'

'Why? It's like my imaginings. Why is everyone so against them?'

'It's unhealthy, Rosemary.'

'Do *you* think so, Gran?'

'It leads to trouble. Now, go and get on with your EduCom.'

'Yes, Gran.'

'Who needs to dream about the past when there's a lovely holograph of a sandy beach to view, eh?'

I didn't believe her, because there used to be a sparkle in Gran's eye. And it wasn't there any more.

My homework question was still on the VDU, unanswered. At the top of the screen flashed a message:

THINK CAREFULLY ROSEMARY!

But my only thoughts were of Gran, of Gran's relics, of Great-Gran Samantha and the Elizabethans. I wondered how Elizabethan children managed to do EduCom, when according to Gran, they studied in large rooms with twenty or thirty other children. There were not enough children on Taurus to justify an EduUnit, so we all worked at home on-line to the EduFactBank. Yawn. Bore.

THINK CAREFULLY ROSEMARY!

flashed the message on the screen.

'If the current state of Ante-Temporal Technology
.... If the current state of Ante-Temporal Technology .... '

Suddenly I *was* thinking. Not carefully, but crazily. I was thinking of Gran's vase. Why worry about getting her another one when there was a perfectly simple way of getting the original back—and the photograph, too. A perfectly simple way, but an illegal and very dangerous way: using 'Ante-Temporal Technology' which is technical jargon for time-spinning.

I could use Mum and Dad's SpaceCruiser. Properly programmed it would spin me through time back to 1990; back to Turnbury. And properly programmed, it would spin me home again, to the European Space Colony (Taurus IV), 2090. With a little time slippage, of course.

THINK CAREFULLY ROSEMARY!

flashed the screen.

Think carefully? I had done with thinking carefully. I had to get the photograph. I had to get the vase. I had to spin through time to 1990. And while I was there, I would skateboard and swim; I would race an

Elizabethan bicycle down a steep hill; I would use my nose to smell things and I would taste fishes' fingers. Just like Gran had said.

I was shivering from head to foot. I wasn't sure whether it was from excitement. Or from fear.

I was going to be a Time Spinner.

5
Plan

'I don't know where she gets it from,' muttered Dad to Mum. 'She' being me.

'Gets what?' muttered Mum back.

'That stubborn streak of hers.'

'Well, don't look at me.'

'Well, it's certainly not from my side of the family. Still, she does seem to have changed her tune since yesterday.'

'Oh, a day's a long time at that age.' 'That age' being twelve.

'I just wish your blessed mother would stop encouraging her.' 'Your blessed mother' being Gran.

'I told her this morning, it's got to stop. Otherwise we'll all be in trouble with the authorities. Oh, I didn't see you there, dear.'

They didn't know I'd been listening.

'Your dad was just saying how perky you looked.'

They didn't know what I was planning.

Actually, there isn't a lot of planning required for spinning in time. In fact, all I needed was Mum and Dad's SpaceCruiser.

'Dad . . . ?'

'Yes, Rosemary?'

'Can I take the SpaceCruiser out for a spin tonight?'

'I see no reason why not. It will have to be a quick one though. Your mother and I are going round to the Wilkinses later. Twenty minutes.'

'Oh, I won't be long, Dad. I've got my homework to do before bedtime, after all.' My most sincere voice.

I did a quick mental reckoning: allowing for time slippage, twenty minutes would give me about eight hours on earth.

'A spin out will do her good,' said Mum to Dad.

I beamed a big smile.

Mum looked severe. 'Haven't you forgotten something, Rosemary?'

'Eh?'

'A word of thanks, perhaps . . . ?'

'Oh sorry. Grats, Mum. Grats, Dad.'

'I should think so, too.'

And that was that. I went into my BedCube, took off my all-white domestic jump suit and put on my all-white traveller jump suit.

I had piloted the SpaceCruiser millions of times. It is dead simple. Everything is faultproof and everything is automatic. Nothing can go wrong.

But the palms of my hands were sweaty with fear and my legs were shaking with panic.

For two very good reasons.

One: nobody cares two zagbrens about a twelve-year-old girl taking a SpaceCruiser out for a spin around the colony. Nobody cares two zagbrens about a twelve-year-old girl taking a SpaceCruiser for a spin to Aquarius. That would be no different from a twelve-year-old Elizabethan taking a ride down the road on a bike. But a twelve-year-old girl taking a SpaceCruiser for a time spin; that is something else. It is strictly illegal. Just like keeping relics is illegal. The penalty if you are caught spinning back in time without permission is immediate transportation to a Space Detention Colony about fifteen galaxies away.

And two; I hate long journeys. I get spin sick. And there was no way I could access the BodiCare

Program and get it to dispense me a couple of QueasiTabs without Mum or Dad seeing me.

So I sauntered down the walkway towards the Domestic Living Unit's decompression chamber door, trying to look relaxed, but already my stomach was churning.

'Just a moment, Rosemary!' Mum's voice behind me. Firm. I froze. Did she suspect something?

'Don't forget your cushion,' she said.

'Oh. Ta.' Relief. I need a cushion to reach the control board in the SpaceCruiser.

'And don't be late back! We're going out, remember!'

'Yes, Mum.'

I looked in on Gran.

'See you, Gran.'

She smiled. Then she whispered, 'Good Luck!' and winked at me. Could she really know what I was planning?

I climbed through the decompression door and walked along the long, white, bright walkway tube to where the SpaceCruiser was anchored. Then I marched through the connecting chamber and into the SpaceCruiser cab itself.

The cab is small. Just enough room for two people. I put my cushion on one of the seats by the control desk, slid up onto it and tapped in the code A-TT into the SpaceCruiser Database.

ACKNOWLEDGED
ANTE-TEMPORAL TRAVEL? CONFIRM!

I tapped in the code: Y.

ACKNOWLEDGED
PROCEED

My lips were dry. I took a deep breath and tapped in the detailed instructions: Dateline: Thursday 29 March 1990. Place: Turnbury Middle School, England. Time of arrival: 1130 hours.

I waited for the SpaceCruiser to move away from its anchorage. But nothing happened. Instead a loud buzzer sounded and a red light flashed above me.

WARNING!

The screen read

YOU HAVE PROGRAMMED FOR ANTE-TEMPORAL TRAVEL.
UNAUTHORISED ANTE-TEMPORAL TRAVEL IS STRICTLY FORBIDDEN AND CARRIES A MAXIMUM PENALTY OF SPACE PENAL COLONY TRANSPORTATION.
DO YOU STILL WISH TO PROCEED?

My hands felt clammy as I typed in the code: Y.

There was a sudden rushing in my head that

seemed to pull the inside of my ears out, and then suddenly I was spinning. Spinning through space. Spinning through time. Spinning to Turnbury, 1990. To meet Great-Gran Samantha. The very best footballer of them all.

6
Bicycle House

A journey through time, of course, cannot be measured in hours and minutes. Suddenly, you are just . . . there. Like in a dream that begins in one place and suddenly moves you somewhere else. And the best thing is, I discovered—there's no time to get spin sick.

And so it was that I found myself hurtling out of a clear blue sky, towards the Elizabethan earth. There was a sharp jolt, and the screen flashed up a new message:

DESTINATION ADJACENT!

I was hovering about a hundred metres over Turnbury Middle School. Inside the SpaceCruiser bleepers were bleeping, buzzers were buzzing and lights were flashing: the automatic landing equipment was seeking out a suitable anchorage. The SpaceCruiser drifted over the school in a slow, deliberate curve before dropping silently and gently towards a small, green carpet just a few hundred metres away from the main building. I peered through the cabin window, searching the ground for some sign of an Elizabethan person, but the whole

area seemed to be deserted.

The SpaceCruiser door slid open. And then—and then I'm not sure what order exactly it all happened. I remember my ears being bombarded with whistling and hammering and ringing and screaming and roaring and my eyes stinging with the glare of sunlight. Then my nose began to fill with incredible sensations, so much so that it seemed as if my head was swelling, bursting, and that any moment it might explode. I clamped my hands over my ears in terror. I fought desperately to catch my breath. Then:

'A-a-a-a-t-t-t-c-c-h-h-h-o-o-o!'
Then:

'A-a-a-a-t-t-t-c-c-h-h-h-o-o-o!' Again.

42

My eyes were streaming with tears. But at least I could breathe again. I leant back in the pilot seat, my eyes closed, my hands half over my ears, trying to accustom myself to these strange surroundings.

When I finally managed to summon up enough energy to step out of the SpaceCruiser, the carpet under my feet felt very rough. I looked down and saw that it wasn't a carpet at all, but millions of tiny flat, pointed, green stalks, sharp as blades, woven all together and rooted into the very ground itself.

As I looked about me, I saw that on three sides of the carpet were long low houses without doors or windows or indeed any sides at all; just roofs. To my amazement, these little houses were full of what I had only seen two-dimensional pictures of before in Gran's old book relics—small, shining, Elizabethan bicycles! Hundreds of them!

There were red bicycles, blue bicycles, yellow bicycles, silver bicycles. Solid bicycles with huge black tyres; bicycles glistening with sleek, shining wheels; bicycles beaming with glowing stripes; bicycles wrapped in golden stars; bicycles with hooters; bicycles with bells. While I was staring at these wonderful machines, I became aware of voices on the other side of the bicycle houses. I moved to the end of the bicycle house and peered round. Two boys, dressed in colourful ragged jackets and dull ragged trousers were facing a smaller boy, who was also

dressed in ragged jacket and trousers.

'I'll get you some tomorrow, Barry,' said the small boy.

'Tomorrow isn't good enough, is it, Reesie?' said one of the large boys to the other large boy.

'No, Barry,' said the other large boy.

'You know our methods,' said this Barry and he lifted the small boy up by the collar of his jacket.

'Ow!' said the small boy. Suddenly I felt another head explosion coming on.

'A-a-a-a . . . . t-c-c-h-h-h-h-o-o-o!' I went.

I tried to duck out of the way, but they heard me and all spun round, the small boy still dangling by his collar from Barry's clenched hand.

'Get her, Reesie!' yelled Barry.

Out of the corner of my eye, I saw Reesie lumbering towards me; Barry—still grasping the small boy—followed him. They charged round the end of the bicycle house and onto the green carpet that wasn't a carpet, right in front of me.

'Good morning,' I smiled. 'I wonder if you can help me. Only, I've just landed. I'm on an ante-temporal excursion from Taurus'—I indicated the SpaceCruiser—'and I'm looking for my Great-Gran Samantha. You might know her. She's the best footballer in Turnbury.'

The boy called Barry dropped the small boy and started shaking. I noticed that his face was very white.

'Ow!' said the small boy.

The boy called Reesie was making a kind of gurgling sound in his throat. His face was very white, too. As white as the ceiling of my BedCube at home.

Suddenly Reesie and Barry turned and ran.

'Aaargh!' yelled Barry, as he struck his ankle on the corner of the bicycle house.

The small boy still stood, staring at me. Then he looked at the SpaceCruiser.

'Are you doing a film?' he enquired.

'No, I'm Rosemary Jemima Martin,' I replied, slowly.

He stared at me a little longer. Then he poke

his tongue.

'Going to tell Miss Piggy of you.'

And he ran off towards the school buildings. Leaving me thinking that these Elizabethans were very strange people indeed.

7
Greg

Red bicycles, blue bicycles, yellow bicycles. My eyes
kept being drawn towards them. And to one in
particular. It was bright yellow, with gleaming
steering handle and wheels. I squeezed myself into
the bicycle house and gently eased the shining
machine out into the walkway. I grabbed hold of the
steering handle grips and began trotting along with
the machine. I swung my leg over the seat just like
I'd seen in Gran's old book relics. I was well away
from the bicycle house by now. I pushed at the
ground with my foot and suddenly I was moving.

Everything on the bicycle started twisting and
wobbling; I leant this way and that. I struggled
desperately to keep upright, but it was no good. I
crashed to the ground, and the magnificent machine
toppled over on top of me.

'Hey you! What are you doing with my bike?' A
voice yelled out from somewhere above my head.

I looked up between the spokes of the spinning
bicycle wheel. A boy stood there, dressed in the same
sort of colourful ragged jacket and dull ragged
trousers as the others who had run away. He wasn't
looking at me, but was anxiously inspecting his

bicycle for damage.

'It's more like what your bicycle's done to me,' I complained. 'I'm injured.'

'That's your fault. That's what happens to people who touch my bike.'

I liked this Elizabethan boy even less than the others I had met.

'Take your stupid bicycle. It doesn't work properly anyway.'

'It did before you got hold of it.'

'No it didn't. It falls over. I bet if you let go of it, it'd fall over.'

The boy looked strangely at me, down his nose.

'You are *weird*,' he concluded.

'And you are stupid.' My leg hurt where the bicycle had fallen on it.

'And why aren't you wearing the school colour— are you new?'

'I don't go to your stupid school. I wish I'd never come here in the first place. I think all you Elizabethans are stupid and all I've got since I arrived is an injured leg and constant head e-e-e-e-xplosions-s-s-s a-a-a-a-chooooo!' I exploded.

The boy frowned at me. He was a little shorter than me, with brown freckles all over his face and untidy hair. 'Are you from London, or something?' he asked and started pushing his machine back towards the bicycle house. I hopped after him, rubbing the

48

throbbing in my leg.

'No, I'm not!'

'It's just that white suit thing you've got on, I thought it might be the latest fashion for girls.'

'I am not from London. I am from the European Space Colony Taurus.'

'You're a time-traveller?'

'I'm a Time Spinner,' I said in a withering voice. 'I've just arrived. In my mum and dad's SpaceCruiser. There.'

We rounded the bicycle house onto the green carpet that wasn't carpet. The boy stared at the SpaceCruiser; then looked at me and frowned.

'It's a bit small, isn't it?'

'It got me here, didn't it?' I replied, tetchily. 'Anyway, Dad's getting a new one with his job next year.'

'You can't leave it there,' said the boy.

'Oh, who says?'

'Because when the bell goes for dinner, then everyone will be all over it.'

'Eh?'

'Look. When Mrs Gascoigne first turned up in her four-wheel drive Suzuki jeep, do you know what happened? Melissa Freebury got her chocolatey fingers all over the leather seats and Martin Dennis got a rounders bat stuck up the exhaust trying to see how big it was. And this is better than a Suzuki jeep.'

The detail of what this Elizabethan boy was saying didn't make much sense to me, though I could catch his general drift: Elizabethans would find my SpaceCruiser much more interesting than their bicycles.

'I'll move it,' I said.

'Send it back a few hours with your remote control facility,' the boy suggested.

'You know all about ante-temporal technology?' I asked, surprised.

The boy nodded. 'Oh yes. I learnt all about it from a book I've been reading: *Strange Visitors from Outer Space* by Henrick Von Nost. Science Fiction.'

I thought: 'He might be objectionable, but at least this Elizabethan boy isn't quite as stupid as the others.' And then he said:

'Are you an alien?'

I was right. He wasn't as stupid as the others. He was more stupid than the others. I raised my eyebrows at him.

'Do I look like an alien?'

'No.'

'Well then.'

'But some space aliens re-model themselves to look like humans. I saw this film called *Invasion of the Body Snatchers*—'

'I am a human being!' I interrupted him.

He shrugged. 'I only asked.'

I ignored him, and took the remote control facility from my pocket. I tapped in the code to send the SpaceCruiser back eight hours. The SpaceCruiser shook, shuddered and then slowly vanished on the spot.

'Wow!' said the boy. For some moments, he stared at the spot where the SpaceCruiser had stood. Then he turned to me.

'Look, I've got to get back to Mr Dixon. I only saw you because I had to take the register over to the office. It's dinner time in half an hour; I'll see you then. You had better stay around here, out of the way.'

'Why?'

'Why? Have you any idea what it's like in school when the bell goes for dinner?'

I shrugged. 'It wouldn't bother me.'

'It would.'

'I *have* spun through time, you know,' I pointed out, trying not to sound too superior.

'But you've never been in Turnbury School when the bell goes for dinner, have you? It's murder.'

Not only were Elizabethans stupid. They were wet. The boy went on:

'I'll teach you to ride my bike, if you like.'

Now he was talking.

'Grats!'

'Providing you let me have a go in your SpaceCruiser.'

There's always a catch.

He was wheeling his bicycle back into the bicycle house. He turned and looked at me hard. 'My name's Greg, by the way.'

I thought for a moment. 'I'm Rojema,' I said, using the name I used in my imaginings.

'Rojema? That's a great name,' he said. 'All the girls in this school are called Kate or Emma.'

'Oh.'

Then he made a grimace. 'Except Samantha Trott, of course.'

My heart missed a beat.

'Er . . . Samantha Trott,' I repeated, trying not to

sound too interested. 'That *is* an unusual name.'

'Unusual? It's unique,' snorted Greg.

'Do you know Great-Gr—er . . . this Samantha girl?' I asked in a couldn't-care-less voice.

'*Everyone* knows Samantha Trott,' Greg tutted. He raised his eyebrows in a strange way. I was desperate to ask him about Samantha Trott, but just at that moment I felt yet another head explosion coming on.

'Aa-a-a-a-choooo!' I went. The whole of my body shook and my eyes streamed tears.

'Bless you!' grinned Greg and ran off in the direction of the school buildings.

Bless you. So that was the name the Elizabethans gave to the awful head explosions.

I sat down on the green carpet where the SpaceCruiser had landed. It felt damp to touch. I thought I might try smelling it, but I didn't want to bring another head explosion on, so I simply lay right back and looked up at the blue, blue sky. The billowing white clouds seemed to stand out like huge and distorted old faces and their shapes kept changing, ever so slowly. It was so much better than the holographs I had seen on Taurus.

Then my eyelids grew heavy and I felt myself drifting off into a deep sleep.

8
Tears

When I woke up, it was still quite quiet. Just a rushing sound in the distance, and a low buzz coming from the school buildings. I had no idea how long it would be before Greg came back.

I got up. My legs and bottom felt damp all over. And my all-white traveller jump suit wasn't quite so all-white any more. I walked up three steps towards the school buildings. These steps were greyish, and they were rough to touch, too. And as for the school buildings—well, blotchy is the only word for them. They weren't smooth, bright white, like the Domestic Living Units on Taurus, but patches of different shades and textures all over.

A door was open and I walked in. It was a horrible sight. It reminded me of scenes of the Great Destruction of 2041 I'd seen on the holograph at home. The ceiling was a dirty white, the floor was grey with black marks all over it and the walls were a blotchy pale blue. On one wall there was a row of pegs on which hung various bits of coloured rough Elizabethan costume. On the opposite wall, there hung many pieces of paper. A chair with three legs had been pushed into the farthest corner.

I went over to the wall with the bits of paper hanging from it. The biggest piece of paper in the middle of the wall was headed FOOTBALL. Football! I studied the large sheet of paper to see if it revealed any details of the Turnbury Girls' match. All it said was FOOTBALL: 29 3 90 1ST XI V ST PATS RC 3 30 K.O. If I was going to get to meet Great-Gran Samantha and get another photograph of the football teams for Gran, let alone find a replacement relic vase, I needed to be able to crack this cryptic shorthand.

Before I had time to get my mind around the odd letters and figures, I became aware that the low buzz of noise in the background had gradually grown louder and more urgent. Suddenly I felt very frightened. I knew something must be about to happen; I didn't know what, but I knew I wouldn't like it; I knew it could be dangerous. I made a frantic dash for the doorway, just as the whole place shook with a deafening clanging that reverberated around the walls and over my head. I covered my ears in panic and ran as fast as I could, but before I could reach the door, hundreds of shouting, screaming Elizabethan school children spilled out of doors and corridors, swarming, shoving, pushing past me in a heaving, grubby throng. My heart was pounding. I could see no way out. The laughing, screaming, shouting and yelling echoed all round my head. In blind panic, I kicked against the mighty surge of bodies, desperate to reach the safety of the far corner. Then my ankle caught on the three-legged chair and I fell into a heap on to the floor.

Almost at once, an arm came at me out of the crowd and grabbed at my wrist.

'Rojema!' bellowed the voice at the end of it.

I found myself hauled to my feet.

'Get me out of here, Greg!' I screamed. 'Get me out!'

Greg pulled me through the crowds. Nobody took much notice. Everyone was busy pulling on their colourful coats and shouting at each other and trying to push their way out of the building. Greg hauled me towards a white door.

'Now get in there, and wait until it quietens down. Lock yourself in. You can't have everybody asking questions.'

'But—'

'No buts! This is *my* territory, Rojema. I *know* what it's like! Now quickly! I'll be waiting out here.'

And he pushed me in. Inside it was white, like a cube on Taurus. There were small watering bowls along one wall with mirrors above. Three girls stood there; their backs to me. Against the opposite wall was a series of doors leading to tiny square rooms, with walls that didn't quite reach the ceiling. I made a dash for one of these tiny rooms and bolted the door behind me.

I was alone with a very primitive MultiFlush. I could hear the voices of the girls by the watering bowls.

'What about Barry, then?'

'When he came in, he apologised for being late. *Apologised*!'

'And he never answered Mrs Harris back once.'

'And he offered to collect the books in at the end.'

'Had he been to see Miss Piggy?'

'No.'

'Well, he'd seen something. He was white as a sheet.'

'Reesie was as bad. His eyes were all glazed.'

'That's normal with him. He watches telly till two o'clock in the morning.'

I couldn't stop shaking and I was still fighting for breath. I was still damp from where I'd lain down on the rough green carpet by the bicycle house. I felt hungry; I wanted my BodiCare Program. I wanted a clean traveller jump suit. I hated the Elizabethan smells, their roughness and their coarse costumes. I hated bossy Greg. I wished I'd never bothered about Gran's stupid relic or her silly photographs.

Suddenly I felt a bless you coming on.

'A-a-a-a-a-chooo!'

It was more than I could bear. I burst into tears.

The three girls had stopped talking. I held my breath. I heard some whispering going on. Then one of them spoke through the door.

'You all right?'

'Yes.' I sobbed.

'You sure?'

'Yes. You heard. Just leave me alone. Just go away!'

'All right. Only asked.'

Then she spoke to her friend.

'Come on, Kate.'

'Who is it, in there?'

'Oh, I don't know. Probably some dopey first year.'

Then the door slammed and all was quiet.

9
Names

As I went to pull back the bolt on the MultiFlush cubicle, I suddenly thought I heard a small cough. My heart missed a beat. Quietly, I reached up to the top of the MultiFlush cube door and pulled myself up off the ground until I could see over the top. A girl stood at one of the watering bowls, looking intently into the mirror. She had reddish hair, like mine. I couldn't see her face. She must have come in as the other girls had gone out. I slid quietly down on the ground. Then I heard footsteps and the door slammed again.

This time I was sure everyone had gone. I slid back the bolt and looked round. It was empty. I peered into one of the mirrors above the watering bowls. My eyes were pinkish and swollen. My all-white jump suit was all-grey and covered with bright green marks where I had lain on the bicycle house carpet. I was beginning to look like an Elizabethan.

I looked around for a ClensuWipe, then remembered that the Elizabethans splashed water from the watering bowl tap onto themselves. I put my head under the tap and turned it on. The water was so cold, like ice; it made me catch my breath. I jumped

back with a yell.

There was a quiet knocking on the door. And Greg called:

'Rojema! You all right in there?'

I rushed out of the door and it was Greg's turn to step back.

'What have you done? Your face and your hair—it's all soaking!'

'I felt hot and sticky, so I watered my face.'

'You mean you *washed* your face.'

'Eh?'

'Never mind. What did you do, put your head under the tap or something?'

'That's right.'

'Well, you're still dripping. Don't you wash—er—water yourself where you come from?'

'No, we just do a bit of dabbing around with a ClensuWipe.'

'Wow.'

It's amazing, the silly things that impress Elizabethans.

'Well, I'm going home for dinner. You coming? You must be starving.'

'No . . . . I *am* hungry though.'

'That's what I meant. Come on, it's only round the corner.'

'If your mum won't mind.'

'No. She's okay.'

'Grats. Grats very much.'

On the way out of the school, we collected Greg's bicycle. We took a narrow black path, which was very rough on the feet, then went through a small gate at the back of the school grounds.

'What sort of food do you like?' asked Greg.

I explained about the BodiCare Program.

'You mean you don't *chew* anything at all?'

'No.'

'Wow. So why have you got teeth, if you don't use them?'

'I'd look pretty silly without them, wouldn't I?'

Greg nodded. 'That's true. The bloke who sells the *Gazette* hasn't got any teeth and he spits at you when he talks.'

'There you are then.'

'I suppose it's like your appendix. You don't use that. But you've got it.'

'Yes.'

The roads here were empty and I noticed that the roaring noise I'd heard in the background at the school was growing fainter the further we walked.

'That's the noise of the traffic on the main road that runs by the front of the school,' Greg explained.

'There's no noise at all on Taurus,' I told him. 'Just the occasional swish of a door and the gentle hum of a conditioning fan.'

I stopped and listened to the sounds coming from a row of trees behind the Domestic Living Units.

'Greg, what's that sound?'

'Eh? Oh that. Birds. You get a lot of them around here.'

'What are they doing?'

'Singing and that.'

'I saw some birds once. On a Spectrograph Gran had borrowed. You couldn't hear them singing though, because of the DigiTune in the background. What sort of birds are they?'

'Well, it can be difficult to tell, There are a lot of birds and their songs are all different.'

'That's fants! Like what?'

Greg seemed to be a little uncomfortable.

'Er . . . like the pigeon. That goes sort of cooo cooo . . . .'

'Coooo . . . . Coooo?'

'Yes.'

We listened.

'Those birds aren't pigeons, Greg,' I said.

'Er . . . . No. There's the cuckoo. That goes sort of er . . . cuckoo.'

'Sort of cuckoo?'

'Yes.'

We listened.

'Those birds aren't cuckoos, either, Greg,' I said.

'No.'

'So what are they, then?'

'Er . . . ummm . . . .'

Before I could tell Greg how stupid I thought Elizabethans were, he had pointed to some petrol-driven vehicles parked along the side of the Elizabethans' Domestic Living Units.

'BMW, Fiesta, Mini, Corolla,' he said.

I looked blankly at him.

'That's the names of those cars!'

'You dilt!' I said. 'Elizabethan petrol-driven vehicles don't have names!' This was obviously a joke, to try and cover up how ignorant he was about the names of birds.

'Of course they do. What's your SpaceCruiser called?'

'A SpaceCruiser,' I shrugged.

'Boring,' said Greg.

'Roman chariots didn't have names, did they? So why do Elizabethan petrol-driven vehicles?'

'Cars,' said Greg, sniffily and he tugged at two levers on the steering handle of his bicycle, so that the wheels locked.

We turned off the road and into a path leading to an Elizabethan Domestic Living Unit. Greg pointed to a petrol-driven vehicle that was even more patchy and blotchy than the Turnbury School buildings. Across the back in little letters was its name: 'Morris Marina'. I tried to imagine our SpaceCruiser having a name like 'Morris Marina'.

'My mum's,' said Greg.

'Is this your Domestic Living Unit then?'

'House,' said Greg.

Greg's house had been constructed by placing small red bricks on top of each other in a typical Elizabethan fashion. There were spaces in the walls for a door and for glass windows. By the door was a large number 4.

'And I suppose your house has got a name, too?' I asked in my sarcastic voice; that one I usually saved for Mum.

'Yep,' said Greg. 'There.'

Above the door were two words: 'Whispering Firs'. I shot Greg a puzzled glance.

'The firs are those trees,' explained Greg, pointing to two trees in front of the house. 'And when it's windy they blow about and it's meant to sound like whispering.' Now it was his turn to sound sarcastic.

'Oh,' I said, trying not to splutter with laughter.

'I think it's stupid, too,' Greg replied, very embarrassed. He pushed a small piece of metal into a tiny hole on the edge of the door. Then he turned the piece of metal and the door swung open. He beckoned to me.

'Come on. And wipe your feet on the mat. Or else Mum will go spare.'

My mind was racing. Cuckoos, Morris Marinas and Whispering Firs were all very well, but I was sticking to Greg for one reason only. Somehow I had to get him to lead me to Great-Gran Samantha. The best footballer of them all.

10
Chokers

I remembered about wiping your feet on the mat from the History disk. Though for some reason I thought it was something that only happened in Japan. I sat down on the doorstep and pulled off my boots and my socks. Then I began to rub my feet on the doormat. It was so rough that sharp tingles started to run up from my ankles, all over my body and I started to giggle uncontrollably.

'Prrumph!' I snorted. 'Oooohhh! Eiiiii!'

Greg spun round.

'What are you doing?'

'Wiping my feet on the mat. Like you said. Ooooohhhh!'

'I meant your shoes not your bare feet.'

'Well, if you meant shoes why did you say feet?'

Elizabethans are crazy, I thought. They say wicked when they mean good, starving when they mean hungry and feet when they mean boots. They don't really know what they mean.

'Gregory?' A woman's voice called.

'Yep!' Greg called back. He turned to me. 'You'd better let me do the talking. Right? Don't say a word.'

'Why?'

'You don't know my mum. She's a one-woman Gestapo. She quizzes you until you trip yourself up. You'd be bound to put your foot in it.'

'Do you mean shoe?' I asked in my sarcastic voice.

'No, I mean foot.'

'I thought when Elizabethans said foot they meant shoe.'

'Just leave the talking to me.'

I really hate bossy people.

'But—' I began.

'Pretend you're foreign or something.'

'But—'

Before I could get a word in, Greg's mum appeared behind us.

'Mum,' began Greg, 'this is Rojema.'

Greg's mum looked me up and down with a critical eye.

'Who?'

'Rojema. She's . . . er on a special visit to school. From er . . . .'

The silence went on for ever.

'From abroad?' Greg's mum finally chipped in.

'Yes.' I could hear the relief in Greg's voice.

Greg's mum whispered to him tetchily, 'You might have said. I've only got spaghetti.'

Greg's mum came up close to me and smiled broadly into my face. Then she said, very slowly and very loudly, 'W-E-L-C-O-M-E   J-E-R-O-M-A!' She pointed out of the door. 'N-I-C-E W-E-A-T-H-E-R! F-O-R Y-O-U-R V-I-S-I-T! T-O   T-U-R-N-B-U-R-Y!'

I beamed innocently at her. Greg rolled his eyes around and looked away.

'C-O-M-E O-N T-H-R-O-U-G-H!' yelled Greg's mum at me with a huge smile.

I carried on beaming at her.

'What *is* she wearing?' she hissed at Greg.

'Er . . . it's the uniform where she comes from.'

'Heaven help us.' She looked me up and down again. 'It's filthy. I just hope she's wiped her feet.'

Greg's Domestic Living Unit was every colour and every texture. The floors swam in bright red and

yellow swirls and the walls were a dull and dirty white. The unit furniture was of every shape and size and material. But this was nothing compared to what I saw when I sat down at the table. Straight in front of me, on a shelf attached to the far wall, I saw, not one, but *two* of the priceless glass vase relics, just like the one Gran had, shining all the colours of the spectrum. It was just what I needed to take back to Taurus with me.

'Bon appetit!' smiled Greg's mum. She sounded like a human version of the BodiCare Program. She turned to Greg and whispered secretively, 'You did say she was French, Gregory?'

Gregory sat with his mouth open, not knowing what to say.

'Oui, je parle français, madame,' I said, in perfect French. Everyone's bi-lingual on the European Space Colony Taurus. 'Bon appetit!'

Greg's mum smiled even more broadly at me.

'But, my Eengless she is only leetle,' I continued.

Greg's mum smiled even more broadly. I was winning her over. Perhaps I'd be able to ask about the vase.

'B-U-T Y-O-U T-R-Y!' Greg's mum looked highly impressed. She turned to Greg. 'Which is more than I can get Gregory to do with his French.'

Greg glared at me and kicked my ankle. I smiled sweetly at him and kicked his ankle back.

In front of me, on a dish, were long coils of shiny, soft white things in a thickish, orangey-red goo. It all reminded me of diagrams I had viewed on the Biology disk. Knowing that Elizabethans ate fishes' fingers, I began wandering what part of what animal this was, lying coiled up on a dish in front of me. Then I wished I hadn't because my stomach turned itself over. Spaghetti, spaghetti—it certainly sounded as if it might be part of something's insides.

I saw Greg lift a pile of the coils onto one of those deadly Elizabethan eating-weapons with four prongs. The pile of coils slipped into his mouth and he started moving his jaws up and down, up and down. Chewing.

Well, I don't know how to chew, and I certainly wasn't going to use one of those Elizabethan eating-weapons. I stared at the dish of coils in front of me, wondering just what my next move ought to be.

Then I noticed that Greg had stopped chewing. He gawped at me in horror. He had remembered my ignorance of Elizabethan eating habits and realised the dilemma I was in.

'Mum—'

'Don't speak with your mouth full, Gregory. Not in front of visitors.'

'But Mum, I think Rojema would prefer some-thing like er . . . soup.'

'Well I'm sorry, Gregory, I haven't got any soup.'

But the longer I stared at the dish of coils, the more I realised that there was an easy solution to the problem. I bent down right over my dish of coils and sucked. Hard.

It took me by surprise, taste. The coils didn't have any effect, they were just warm and flabby, but when the red goo reached my lips, my whole mouth lit up like fireworks. All round my gums and under my tongue was sparkling, fizzing, tingling. And then amongst the mouth-fireworks bubbled a flood of spit. I tried hard to suck, to breathe, to swallow, to suck some more. But all I could do was choke. I couldn't

help what happened next. It was all perfectly natural.
I opened my mouth to try and catch my breath and
the whole lot, coils, goo and spit came sliding and
dripping out onto the dish in front of me.

Greg's mother's eyes sort of popped out of her
head. It was as if somebody had called her a rude
word. Then she started choking too, her beaming
smile suddenly transformed into a mixture of horror
and disgust. Next Greg started choking, his worried
face transformed into a mixture of laughter and tears.

'For goodness' sake fetch her a glass of water or
something,' Greg's mum hissed.

When Greg came back she muttered, half to him
and half to herself: 'If this is what the French have

got to teach us, then we were all better off out of the Common Market. They're just the same at bus stops, you know.'

I managed to suck a few more of the spaghetti coils into my mouth, but not many. It takes much longer to get through an Elizabethan dinner than it does to gulp down a few tablets from the BodiCare Program dispenser. In fact, it was almost ten minutes before Greg and his mum finished their coils. All the time, I could feel Greg's mum glaring at me.

And all the time, the glass vase on the shelf winked at me; out of reach, now, for sure.

I was mighty glad to get out of Greg's Domestic Living Unit. We were in the doorway when Greg stopped abruptly and called back to his mum:

'Mum, my football kit!'

'In the airing-cupboard. Where else?' yelled Greg's mum. Although she was somewhere way beyond the KitchenCube, she still sounded furious.

But I didn't care. For Greg had uttered two wonderful words. Football kit! Greg was in the Turnbury Boys' football team.

And if I tagged along with Greg to the football match, I would get to meet Great-Gran Samantha.

11
Skid

Greg was pushing his bicycle along, and kicking a dented can along the path at the same time, his eyes pinned firmly on the ground.

'Why did you decide to come to Turnbury?' he asked.

I looked at Greg. He was the best chance I'd got of doing what I most wanted to do in the whole, entire world and universe—meeting Great-Gran Samantha. I would have to try and explain. I took a deep breath.

'You know you said everyone in your school was called Emma or Kate, except for Samantha Trott . . . . '

'Snotty Sam?'

'Eh?'

'Snotty Sam. That's what we call her. She's the bossiest person ever born and she thinks she's Mastermind—'

The anger welled up inside me. The stupid little ignorant Elizabethan! How dare he talk about my great-gran like that!

'She's the best footballer of them all!' I shouted at him.

'Huh, *she* thinks she is. Everyone else thinks she's

77

yuk. You saw her, didn't you? No I suppose you didn't. You were hiding.'

'What do mean?' I asked quickly, trying to hide the excitement in my voice.

'When you were in the girls' toilet. She came in. Before you came out.'

'What . . . ?' I remembered the red-headed girl I had peered at over the MultiFlush door. 'A red-headed . . . . '

'Ginger. That's her.'

'That was Samantha . . . . ' My voice trailed off. I could hardly bear to think of it. I had actually seen Great-Gran Samantha, but I hadn't realised it.

Greg stopped suddenly and looked at me, hard. 'Why? What's Snotty Sam got to do with you?'

'Oh nothing . . . nothing at all . . . ' I lied. I couldn't tell him about Great-Gran Samantha now. I just couldn't.

We had reached the small gate that led to the small path up to the school and so I quickly changed the subject.

'Hey Greg, teach me to ride on your bicycle! Go on, you said you would . . . . '

'Oh, all right.'

'Grats!'

'But you've got to give me a go in your SpaceCruiser!'

'Later . . . !'

I swung my leg over the bicycle seat.

'Right,' said Greg. 'Now put your feet on the pedals.'

'The what?'

Greg placed my feet on the pedals.

'Now push with your feet. I'll hold the back of the saddle until you get going.'

I pushed, first gently, then harder, I felt it pulling in my legs.

'Greg, has it got an in-built automatic speed regulator?'

Already the faces of startled Elizabethan children were beginning to flash by me.

'Greg,' I yelled, 'how does this bicycle of yours stop?'

No answer.

'Greg!'

I glanced over my shoulder. Greg was nowhere to be seen. The air was rushing about my ears and all the time I seemed to be going faster. I thought: if I am injured how will I get back to the SpaceCruiser? I thought: if I die, how will I get back to Taurus? I thought: I don't want to die. I looked down at the bicycle; I had learnt just how stupid the Elizabethans were; I knew that nothing on the machine was going to be automated. There were all sorts of rods and levers. Suddenly I recalled Greg's antics when he was wheeling his bicycle home before dinner. I squeezed one of the levers that was attached to the steering handle. Instantly, the back wheel locked, I lurched forward, clouds of dust were thrown up behind me and I came to a standstill. A few children gawped in amazement. This is fun, I thought.

I pedalled hard some more, gathering speed down a small hill that led to the bicycle house. Sounds whistled and hissed through my ears and smells wafted past my nose. I pedalled furiously towards the green carpet in front of the bicycle house. Right in the middle were Reesie and Barry, sitting on top of the small boy they had been threatening when I had landed.

'Yeoowww!' I yelled. And squeezed the wheel-locking lever as hard as I could. Reesie and Barry looked up, frozen in terror. The back wheel of the bicycle squealed, then locked, cutting a long brown line in the green carpet. I came to a halt, about twenty centimetres from Reesie's face.

'It's her again,' whimpered Reesie.

'Hello, Reesie,' I grinned.

They were already up and backing away from me.

'She called you Reesie, Reesie,' said Barry. 'She knows your name.'

And they were off up the steps before I could explain. The small boy they had been sitting on stood his ground for a bit, then said to me:

'I'm going to tell Miss Piggy of you.'

And he ran off. Just as he had done before. You would have thought that he would have been grateful to me for rescuing him again.

I climbed off the bicycle seat, just as Greg came panting up behind me.

'You—phew—I mean—phew—where did you learn to skid like that?'

I shrugged. 'I don't know. It just sort of happened.'

'You were pretty amazing.'

'Wicked?' I asked.

'Really wicked,' he replied.

'It was fants.'

Skid, I thought. Good Elizabethan word that.

The bell rang in the school.

'How long are you staying?' asked Greg. He was checking all the levers and rods on his bicycle.

'Well, current ante-temporal technology is only advanced enough to allow me to stay on Earth for about eight hours.'

'Why's that?'

'For every hour I spend here, I lose about two and a half minutes of Taurus time. The SpaceCruiser's got to be back for my mum and dad in twenty minutes of Taurus time. . . . . '

'Eight hours of Turnbury time . . . . '

'Yes. Which means that I've got to re-access the SpaceCruiser at about half past seven this evening.'

Greg took a deep breath. 'If you like you could come and watch the football after school.'

My heart missed a beat.

'I suppose I could,' I said, in a couldn't-care-less voice. Knowing that nothing, but nothing, would stop me being there.

'Great! I'm in goal and you owe me a go in your SpaceCruiser anyway and I'm going to work out a lot of questions in Maths about the future to ask you—'

All I was worried about was the football.

'What time does it start?'

'Three thirty. Straight after school.'

'I'll see you here, then.'

'All right, and if you go wandering about, be careful. If any of the teachers spot you, you'll be hauled off for not wearing the school colour.'

'School colour? What's that?'

'Mauve.'

'Mauve?'

Greg ran off towards the school building, paused, then turned.

'Oh and you can meet Snotty Sam, too.'

'Really . . . ' I shrugged in a disinterested voice.

'Yes, she'll be playing for the girls. You'll see how obnoxious she is.' He paused. 'How come you know about her, Rojema?'

I shrugged. 'Just something I heard,' I said, truthfully.

'And another thing, Rojema.'

'What?'

'Promise not to touch my bike.'

'Cross my heart and hope to die,' I said, in a sarcastic voice.

Greg frowned, shook his head and ran off into the school.

12
Miss Piggy

This time I wasn't going to get damp from lying on the rough green carpet by the bicycle house, so when it was all quiet, I wandered into the school building and sat down on the floor under the wall with pieces of paper pinned to it.

With only three hours between the end of the football game and the time I should be thinking of re-accessing the SpaceCruiser, I wasn't going to have long to get everything done. But I reckoned it was possible, providing I planned it all properly. Yes, planning was what was needed and so I began to think everything out in detail.

After thinking everything through carefully in my head, this was how the plan began to look: Greg would take me to the football match. I would then be able to meet Great-Gran Samantha. I would explain to her who I was and she would help me get a relic vase and a photograph of the football team, to take back to Gran. Greg wouldn't want to hang around with me, if I was talking to Great-Gran Samantha, because he thought she was bossy (he could talk), so that would save awkward problems over my promise to let him have a go in the

SpaceCruiser.

I tucked my knees up under my chin and sucked on my nostrils to try and get a smell of the school. I wished I hadn't. It wasn't very pleasant. Then, all of a sudden, I became aware of a pair of feet on the floor in front of me. I looked slowly up and saw a pair of ankles, then a dark blue Elizabethan skirt, then a body and a face. I had no doubt that I was looking at a Turnbury Middle School Teacher. She was quite young and she had a lot of that face-paint the Elizabethans used, around her eyes and all over her mouth. She peered at me over the top of a pair of those funny Elizabethan sight-aids they used to put on their noses, before eyeball transplant surgery was invented. She didn't look very pleased.

'Just what do you think you're doing?' she snapped.

It wasn't the sort of snap you argued with.

'Smelling the school,' I answered, truthfully.

The sight-aid slipped down her nose.

'Get up!' she glared.

It wasn't the sort of glare you argued with. I got up.

'What do you think you're wearing?'

'What I always wear when I'm out. My all-white traveller jump suit.'

'And what is the Turnbury School colour?'

I knew the answer to this one.

'Mauve,' I answered; rather pleased with myself.

'Which is not the same as all-white, is it? Particularly an all-white that looks more like an all-grey.'

And I knew the answer to this one.

'No.'

'What is your name, young lady?'

I knew the answer to this one, too. I thought it best to play safe. 'Jemima,' I replied in a meek sort of voice. My middle name. No lie.

There was a pause as the Turnbury School teacher looked me up and down.

'And who is meant to be teaching you now, Jemima?'

My mouth went very dry. This one I *didn't* know the answer to.

'Er . . . I . . . .'

Then suddenly I remembered the small boy Reesie and Barry bullied and the name of the teacher he was always going to report me to.

'Miss Piggy.' I almost grinned at her, I was so impressed with my quick thinking.

'I beg your pardon?'

These Elizabethans do seem to get very deaf. I thought. It must be all the roaring of the petrol-driven vehicles, and the screaming and shouting of the children and the awful way it seems to echo round and round the buildings.

'MISS PIGGY!' I repeated, louder.

The teacher seemed to heave herself up about ten centimetres. And her left eye sort of twitched.

'Young lady, I think you had better come with me,' she snapped again.

As I said, it wasn't the sort of snap you argued with. So I followed her.

She walked fast. Past UniCube after UniCube, full of Elizabethan children, grouped around tables, heads down. I thought: somewhere in one of those UniCubes is my Great-Gran Samantha. We stopped at a shiny brown door. HEAD TEACHER said a sign that was pinned on it. I thought, judging by the stupidity of some Elizabethans, they need their heads teaching. Below HEAD TEACHER it said MISS S.J. PIGOTT B.A. A cold shiver ran down my spine.

The teacher held the door open.

'Come in, Jemima.'

Miss S.J.Pigott's UniCube was unlike any of the others that I had glimpsed on my walk through the school building. There was a large table, two-dimensional representations of Elizabethan life on the wall and a spongy, fibrous carpet covering on the floor.

'Sit down,' she said.

The chair was large and comfortable.

'So, you should be in lessons with a'—she paused ever so slightly—'Miss Piggy.' Miss S.J.Piggot looked hard at me.

89

'I think I might have made a mistake,' I blurted out. Coming to this stupid school in the first place, I thought.

'I think you probably have. Firstly because I do not teach any lessons in the afternoons.'

'Oh . . .' I mumbled.

'And secondly, because although I am well aware of the nickname which has been given me by the current generation of Turnbury pupils, it seems to me to require a young person of exceptional rudeness or stupidity to use it to my face.'

If I understood her correctly, it was serious. If Miss Piggy was a nickname used by Turnbury pupils about their Head Teacher, then one thing was certain: it was bound to be rude. I couldn't see much difference between Pig-gy and Pig-ott, but one thing I had already learnt on my brief visit was that Elizabethans are a strange lot. I wished there was a cupboard which I could have crawled into.

'I am sorry, Miss Pigott,' I began, 'I think someone's been playing a practical joke . . . . '

'Oh, so do I,' said Miss S.J.Pigott B.A. quickly. 'The question is, *who?*'

I didn't like her tone.

'Jemima . . . . ' Miss S.J.Pigott B.A. raised an eyebrow. 'You did say that was your name?'

'Yes, Miss Pigott.'

'How extraordinary. You know, you don't *look* a Jemima!'

'No . . . ?'

'No.' Miss S.J.Pigott B.A. leant right across her desk and looked hard into my eyes. 'No, you look like a Rojema to me.'

My heart started pounding. I couldn't believe it. How did she know? Reesie, Barry and the small boy—they didn't know. No one knew, apart from Greg. He wouldn't have, surely? Not Greg?

'Surprised? Ah, I've heard all about you, Rojema.'

'You have?' My voice was very small.

'Yes, I have. Gregory Barrett's mother was on the 'phone to me, just now. Apparently she found your behaviour as primitive and as puerile as I do. So,

91

Rojema Jemima, I'd like a thorough explanation of exactly who you are and what you are doing wandering about Turnbury Middle School.'

Taurus . . . the SpaceCruiser . . . ante-temporal travel . . . Great-Gran Samantha . . . I was sure she wouldn't believe any of it. I couldn't tell her, anyway. I just sat there. Growing hotter and more uncomfortable by the minute.

'Well?'

Silence.

'I could repeat everything I have said to you in French. But unlike Gregory Barrett's mother, I don't for one moment believe that you *are* French.'

Silence.

'I'm waiting, Rojema. And I'm happy to sit here all afternoon, if necessary.'

Miss Piggy sat back, folded her arms, and looked very much as if she meant what she said.

13
Football

All I could do was play for time and hope that somehow, an idea might come to me. I couldn't sit there forever. I'd got a great-gran to meet, relics to collect and I'd got to get the SpaceCruiser back to Taurus in time for Mum and Dad to go to the Wilkinses. It would be best to start with the end and work back, as slowly as I could, I thought. I cleared my throat.

'I am here because ... I am here for the football match this afternoon after school.'

Light shone from Miss Pigott's eyes and her mouth spread into a disagreeable smirk.

'Ah-ha. So that's it, is it?'

'Yes, Miss.'

'I might have known. You're a pupil at St. Patrick's!'

I didn't say yes. And I didn't say no. Miss Piggy leapt up, pushed back her chair and strode purposefully towards a door at the side of the UniCube, opened it and called:

'Miss Ferguson, have you got St. Patrick's number to hand there?'

I needed no second chance. I was up like a shot

and at the window before you could say Miss Piggy. I lifted the catch, flung the window open and jumped. The bushes were rough and sharp, but I picked myself up and ran for all I was worth away from the Head Teacher's luxury UniCube and away from the school.

Eventually I found myself back in the small lane that led to Greg's Domestic Living Unit. I ran up to the top of a small bank from where I could see the school in the distance and sat down under some trees and tried to get my breath and my thoughts back. It wasn't easy. I thought of what Miss Piggy might do—send out a search party, question Greg—and the more I thought, the more I didn't like what I thought.

And that's the way I stayed all afternoon. Looking, worrying; listening, worrying; thinking, worrying. I heard no birds, I didn't even bother to try and smell anything, I was so intent on watching the school.

After an eternity, the school bell clanged. The bicycle house and surrounding pathways swarmed with yelling, screaming, shouting, hurrying figures. It was as if the building was on fire, so quickly did everyone race away from the school. A lot of them rushed by the bottom of the bank where I was sitting, but they were in too much of a dash to notice me, crouched under a tree above them. In no time at all, everything was as quiet as it had been before the clanging of the bell, and the bicycle house and the pathways were empty. Except for one solitary figure waiting by the bicycle house. Greg. He looked this way and that. He inspected his feet. He rubbed a small mark off his bicycle. He looked at the watch he wore strapped to his wrist.

I clambered down the back and ran up the school path, calling him. As soon as I reached the bicycle house, he started.

'I told you to keep out of the school!' He was cross.

'I'm sorry. I did escape.'

'Oh yes, very clever. But not until you'd caused the biggest rumpus since Melissa Freebury brought her pony into assembly.'

'Rumpus . . . ?' I echoed, innocently. I didn't know

exactly what this quaint-sounding Elizabethan term meant, but I had a good idea.

'You know I was sent for? By Miss Piggy!'

'Oh.'

'She grilled me for ages. Who were you . . . what were you doing in school . . . .'

'Oh.'

'I had to pretend I didn't know. In the end she let me off with a rollicking and told me not to pick up strange girls.'

'Oh.'

'And if you think you're going to watch our football match, you've another think coming.'

'Greg! You said!'

'You are trouble. You'd best get back where you came from.'

I had to get to that match. I had to see Great-Gran Samantha. It was desperate, but I knew only one thing would persuade Greg. Bribery.

'I thought you wanted a go in the SpaceCruiser?'

Greg huffed; and puffed.

'All right. But keep out of trouble! Football's a serious business.'

We walked off in the direction of the sports pavilion. It was on the far side of the school, well away from the main buildings and the football pitch was on the far side of that, so I was in no danger of bumping into Miss S.J.Pigott B.A. Besides, according to Greg, she had left school to go to a meeting.

Greg said: 'You didn't really call her Miss Piggy, did you?'

'I don't see why Miss Pig-gy is rude, and Miss Pig-ott isn't.'

Greg beat his hands on his head. Strange people, Elizabethans. Then he explained to me why Miss Pig-gy was rude and Miss Pig-ott was not. And I found I was blushing with the thought of it all.

'And while we're on the subject,' Greg went on, 'why did you tell her your name was Jemima?'

My turn to explain.

'Do you have rude nicknames for people where you come from?' he asked.

'Dilt,' I said.

'Dilt?'

'It means someone who does stupid things without thinking,' I explained.

And Greg gave me a funny look.

'You said it,' he said.

My first impression of the sports pavilion was one of smell. A sweet, cloying smell, that I thought was distinctly unpleasant. Greg left me in the pavilion while he went off to the changing rooms. There were one or two very small boys half hiding in a corner. They nudged each other, giggled and pointed at me.

I didn't mind, because I knew that soon I would be meeting Great-Gran Samantha. My heart was beating fast in anticipation. It was then that I became aware of a bit of a commotion. First a woman came out of the girls' changing rooms. She was dressed all in mauve; her trousers tied at her ankles. She whispered anxiously to one of the small giggling boys. He went into the boys' changing rooms and came out with a man who was dressed exactly the same as the woman. He talked with the woman and they both looked very serious indeed. Then the man went back into the boys' changing room. A few moments later he reappeared with Greg. Greg was dressed in his football kit. He talked with the man and woman. It was then I realised that they were all coming over towards me.

My first thought was that Greg had set me up, that this was a trap, a plan to get me back to Miss S.J.Pigott B.A. My second thought was escape. But Greg and the teachers were between me and the door.

'Here she is,' said Greg, pointing at me. All of a sudden I felt angry and betrayed. How could he do this? Then the woman spoke.

'Rojema?'

I nodded.

'I'm Miss Gascoigne. I run the Turnbury Girls' football team. We've got a bit of a problem and I wonder if you can help us out?'

I looked at Greg. He was grinning.

'It's like this,' Miss Gascoigne went on, 'one of our

team went home ill this afternoon. We're one short. You don't by any chance fancy a game of football, do you? Only Greg here said you might be willing. It doesn't matter that you don't go to Turnbury Middle, it's a Turnbury Junior Youth team, really. It's just the school lets us use their facilities.'

Did I want to play football? The game of all my imaginings? In the same team as my Great-Gran Samantha? Within two minutes, I had changed into a spare set of the mauve Turnbury football kit and had joined the rest of the girls' team on the football pitch. The St.Patrick's team had already arrived. They were all in bright green and white stripes.

Greg was trying to explain the new offside rules to me. I was looking around for Great-Gran Samantha.

'Where's Samantha Trott?' I asked him.

'It's *her* place you've taken. She went home at lunch-time and didn't come back. Sick.'

'But . . . how . . . . '

Had I been through all this for nothing?

'Why *are* you so concerned about Snotty Sam?' asked Greg. Before I had time to answer, Miss Gascoigne blew the whistle and the game was underway.

Football takes a bit of getting used to. The first time I kicked the ball, I swung back my foot and gave it an almighty thump. It went sailing over the goal and hit the wall of the sports pavilion. The second time I found myself with the ball, I tried a smaller kick. All at once, I seemed to have three feet and I ended up tripping over all of them and falling to the ground with a thud. This was a signal for the very small boys who were watching the game to start laughing and giggling again.

The bump and the mud and the scramble helped. I found that the bump didn't kill me. And I found I quite liked the mud and the scramble. Gradually, I began to get a feel for the ball. I began to be able to turn, to feint and to dummy, to tackle, backheel, sidestep, shoot, shout, yell.

'Come on, Roj!' someone would call.

'That's yours, Roj!'

'Where were you, Roj!'

'Roj! You're an elephant!'

'Over here, Roj!'

'Go on, Roj! Go o-o-o-n-n-n, Roj!' The yells this time were more insistent, desperate, imploring and with a mixture of fear and excitement I realised why. In front of me was space. And in front of me was St. Patrick's goalmouth. Their keeper was swinging to and fro and moving fast towards me, hoping to pluck the ball from my feet. I knocked it to one side with my left foot and while it was still rolling, struck it hard with my right towards the goal.

The ball curled ever so slowly through the air, and as it reached the top of its arc it seemed to hang there

for a moment and the keeper rushed back desperately to her line. Then it dropped into the top corner of the net.

Miss Gascoigne blew hard on her whistle and the team were slapping me on the back and hugging me and saying:

'Magic, Roj!'

'Really great, Roj!'

'Great work, Roj!'

And I wished that moment could have lasted for ever.

14
Bottle

'Say cheese!' said Miss Gascoigne and she held an Elizabethan photographic instrument up to her eye.

'Smelly feet!' everyone yelled.

Click, went Miss Gascoigne's photographic instrument.

And suddenly, I knew the truth. It was not Great-Gran Samantha in Gran's photograph of Turnbury Girls' football team: it was me.

'Well played, Rojema,' said Miss Gascoigne as we made our way to the changing rooms. 'And thanks for helping us out. I didn't know how we'd manage without Sam. Look at you! You've managed to get mud everywhere. Still it'll all wash off.'

It was not Great-Gran in the photograph; it was me.

I could think of nothing else as the shower washed over me. Clens u Wipe is a lot simpler than the Elizabethan washing process, which is tedious, messy, inefficient and very wet. But after a warm washing you feel like you've got a new skin somehow. You don't get that with Clens u Wipe.

Outside, the boys' team were joking with Greg. When they saw me approaching, they moved back,

103

laughing and nudging each other, just like the small boys back in the sports pavilion had done. By the time I reached them, they had already begun to move away, leaving Greg standing on his own.

'Watch it, Greg!' they laughed.

'Tell your mum!'

They ran off. Out of sight. They seemed to find something very funny. Strange people, the Elizabethans.

'Eight five to us!' I said. 'And I scored one of them.'

'I let in three,' shrugged Greg. 'Come on, let's grab some fish and chips, I'm starving. My mum gave me some money. I think she was scared I'd bring you home for tea.'

It wasn't Great-Gran Samantha in the photograph; it was me.

I would never meet Great-Gran Samantha, now. That moment had come and gone. And the only chance I had of getting some relics to take back to Taurus for Gran, was by sticking with Greg.

Hundreds of petrol-driven vehicles careered past us as we walked to the fish and chip shop. I coughed and choked and felt a head explosion coming on.

'Atchoooo!'

We turned off the main road and another smell hit my nostrils. It was sharp and bright and I felt the inside of my mouth gathering water.

'Fish and chips,' said Greg. 'Wait here.'

Greg went into the shop and came out carrying two parcels.

'Where shall we eat them?' he asked.

'I know a good place,' I said.

We sat on the green bank, where I had spent the afternoon watching for Miss Piggy. Fish and chips must be the most fants Elizabethan thing ever. For a start, you don't use eating-weapons, you use your hands. And the taste—it is like munching through every colour in the spectrum.

'Not long now,' said Greg.

'Not long now, what?'

'Not long now before you have to access the

SpaceCruiser.'

'No.'

'You never did tell me why you came to Turnbury in the first place.'

'Well . . . ' I didn't quite know what to say, how much to say, how to say it. 'It's a bit complicated . . . . ' I began. I started to tell him about my imaginings; I thought I might as well. After all, Greg wasn't the sort of person who needed convincing.

'And?' said Greg.

He was the only chance I'd got now of taking some relics back to Gran, so I told him about the broken vase and that I'd time spun back to 1990 to get Gran another one. But I said nothing about Samantha Trott.

'But why Turnbury, of all places?'

'Why not?'

'Because nobody just *comes* to Turnbury, there's nothing to come for. If you'd just been coming to Earth for a bit of a lark you'd have gone to somewhere like London or Alton Towers. I reckon you came to Turnbury because you have some sort of link here.'

'One of Gran's relics is that photograph of the Turnbury football team.'

'What, the one that Miss Gascoigne took?'

I nodded. But I said nothing about Samantha Trott.

'Amazing. But—'

'But, Greg. I still haven't got anything for Gran.'

'Let's have a look round.'

It was while we were walking back towards the bicycle house that I spotted it. On a doorstep. A magnificent glass vase, more wonderful than the one of Gran's I had broken. I pointed it out to Greg.

'That? That's only a milk bottle.'

'But it's magic.'

'Take it. No one will mind.'

We walked on in silence. I kept a firm hold of the marvellous milk bottle. I could still taste the fishes and chips on my lips.

'Greg?'

'Yes?'

'Do fishes have fingers?'

Greg tried to stop himself from laughing.

'Fingers? Of course not!'

'My gran said they did.'

'Your gran was wrong.'

The bicycle house was empty, apart from Greg's bicycle.

I accessed the SpaceCruiser and it swished down out of the air in front of us.

'Well, go on, sit in it, then,' I said to Greg. 'I can't let it take you anywhere, though, you'd never get back. And neither would I.'

Greg sat in the tiny cabin. Shaking his head.

'Now I know it's for real,' he said.

He got out and walked around it.

'You can have another go on my bike, if you want.'

'No grats.'

'Have you got to go back?'

I nodded.

'Even though Taurus is boring?'

'Yes. It's where I live, isn't it?'

'Home, you mean?'

'I suppose so.'

'Might you make another trip?'

'I don't know.'

'It's been a great day.'

'Yes. I'm really glad I've got my relic.' I'm really sorry I never met Great-Gran Samantha, I thought.

Greg undid the mauve strip of rough Elizabethan rag that was knotted round his neck.

'Here take this. It's my school tie. For you. Another relic.'

'Grats,' I said. And wished I had something to give to him.

I stepped onto the SpaceCruiser. Greg held out his hand and shook mine, furiously.

'See you,' he said.

'It was all wicked,' I smiled. 'Oh, the photograph. I almost forgot. The photograph of the football teams. Can I have it, so I can return it to Gran's relic box?'

Greg shrugged. 'I haven't got it.'

'But you must have!'

'Not yet. It won't be developed until the end of the week.'

Greg's face bore a puzzled look. Then the buzzer went in the cabin, the door slid shut and with a tremendous thrust the SpaceCruiser spun up into the Earth's atmosphere.

15
Gran's Dad

Ante-temporal slippage meant that in taking eight hours on Elizabethan Earth, I had lost twenty minutes of time on Taurus.

I opened the Unit door and called out:

'Hi Mum. Hi Dad. I'm back!'

'That was quick!' Mum called from the Kitch-Cube.

I dashed into my BedCube. Quickly, I changed into my all-white domestic jump suit; tied up the grubby, creased up traveller jump suit with the neck rag Greg had given me and stuffed the bundle under the bed. Then I slid the milk bottle relic under the bed as well.

I lay down on my bed and stared at the clean, white ceiling. I couldn't work it out. If it was *me* in the photograph and not Great-Gran Samantha, how come she had got a copy which had been passed down the generations to Gran's relic box? Why had the photograph been so important to her?

'Just going round the Wilkinses, dear.' Mum's face beamed at me from the doorway. Her face creased into a frown; then she smiled. 'You look much better for your little spin around the Space Colony, Rosemary. You must do it more often.'

I don't know why, but I wanted to laugh. I bit my lip.

'And you can finish that homework of yours while we're out!'

I waited for the swish of the door. This time I would be careful.

'Hello, dear,' said Gran.

I hugged her for all I was worth.

'Here,' I said, and held out the milk bottle relic.

'Rosemary . . . .' She cleared her throat and tried hard to put on a stern sort of face. 'Rosemary. What you did, in time-spinning like that was very wrong . . . and not right . . . and . . . and—'Suddenly she broke out into gurgles of laughter. 'Good on you girl for doing it!'

'You knew I was going, didn't you!'

'I didn't dare guess. What a magnificent milk bottle!' She held it up to the light. 'I shall treasure it, dear.'

'Gran, I've so much to tell you!'

'I expect you have.'

'About the bicycle house and head explosions and Miss Piggy and—'

'All in good time. You must have felt strange among all those Elizabethan types. What's that bundle you're clutching there?'

'This? Oh, it's my traveller jump suit. And a

present I got of an Elizabethan neck rag.'

'Here, you'd better put that under the bed as well.'

'Thanks, Gran.'

I sat down on Gran's bed and sighed. 'I wish I could've met Great-Gran Samantha, though. I so wanted to see her and and just to talk really. I would have felt like I belonged. But I didn't. The one thing I really wanted to do and I didn't.' I paused. 'And I didn't manage to get a photograph of the football match to replace the one Dad took away—'

'He didn't take the photograph away.'

I could not believe what I was hearing.

'He didn't . . . ?'

'Oh, he took everything else. All my relics, tipped down the MultiFlush except the photograph. You see, as soon as your mum and dad came in the room I slipped the photograph under my bottom. I was sitting on it all the time the row was going on.'

She laughed. But I was still frowning. I had had a dangerous day trying to get a photograph for Gran, which she had all the time.

'May we look at the photograph again?' I whispered.

Gran crawled under her bed. 'I taped it to the underside of my bed, it's safe there, I think.'

I found myself trembling, trying to get the facts, the time and the history right in my head. I looked hard at the photograph. It was the one Miss

Gascoigne took all right. And there I was in the back row.

'Gran, this girl in the back row we thought was Great-Gran Samantha because she looks like me, *is* me. I played in her place.'

'You, Rosemary . . . ? Well, I never did! I said it looked like you, didn't I?'

'But why did Great-Gran Samantha have the photograph, if she wasn't in it?'

Gran's turn to frown. 'I must have got it wrong.'

'Like you did about fishes' fingers,' I muttered under my breath.

Gran didn't hear me. She was smiling. 'No . . . this photograph must have belonged to your great-grandad, not your Great-Gran Samantha. You see, he would have been playing for the boys' football team.'

She studied the line-up of the Turnbury Boys' Football team, holding the photograph close to her eyes.

'There he is! Your great-grandad!'

She was pointing to the goalkeeper.

'Greg . . . ?' I hardly managed to whisper.

'That's right. Your Great-Grandad Greg.'

'Greg . . . was married to Great-Gran Samantha?'

'Yes dear, great-grandads are usually married to great-grans.'

'But . . . .'

But I couldn't find anything more to say at that moment. Images of the time I had spent with Greg kept flashing through my mind. I wished he had known. And then I was glad he hadn't. He would have been really embarrassed; all the things he had said about Great-Gran Samantha—Snotty Sam.

Greg. Great-Grandad Greg. Gran's father Greg. Now that I knew, I felt a sort of sense of my own history; of who I was. Greg and Samantha. Part of me. Somehow I had to hold on to it all; the part of me that was from Turnbury. I got up from Gran's bed.

'Gran. There's a lot to tell you, but it's all a bit

muddled at the moment. But I've decided to type it all up on disk.'

'Good idea. Though it won't be approved of, you know. Not in this day and age. Typing up *stories* is of no use at all to life on Space Colony Taurus, they'll say.'

'Piggies to usefulness,' I said.

Gran blinked.

'I'll keep the disk under your bed, if I can, Gran. You can access it whenever you like.'

'Fine . . . . '

She sighed. 'Rosemary, I hate to have to say this, but you know the first thing your mother will say when she comes in?'

'Yes, Gran,' I sighed.

'She'll say, "Rosemary, have you done that homework?" '

'Well, some things are more important than homework,' I said.

'Rosemary, quite where you get your bossy stubbornness from, I don't know.'

I thought: You may not, but I've got a pretty good idea.

I went into my BedCube and booted up my WordPro.

'ONE. *Imagining*,' I typed. 'It all started with the fishes' fingers . . . . '

Other great reads ⤳ *from* **Red Fox**

Further Red Fox titles that you might enjoy reading are listed on the following pages. They are available in bookshops or they can be ordered directly from us.

If you would like to order books, please send this form and the money due to:

ARROW BOOKS, BOOKSERVICE BY POST, PO BOX 29, DOUGLAS, ISLE OF MAN, BRITISH ISLES. Please enclose a cheque or postal order made out to Arrow Books Ltd for the amount due, plus 75p per book for postage and packing to a maximum of £7.50, both for orders within the UK. For customers outside the UK, please allow £1.00 per book.

NAME_____

ADDRESS_____

_____

Please print clearly.

Whilst every effort is made to keep prices low, it is sometimes necessary to increase cover prices at short notice. If you are ordering books by post, to save delay it is advisable to phone to confirm the correct price. The number to ring is THE SALES DEPARTMENT 0171 (if outside London) 973 9000.

OTHER TITLES YOU MAY ENJOY FROM RED FOX

☐ The Seven Treasure Hunts	Betsy Byars	£2.50
☐ Flossie Teacake's Fur Coat	Hunter Davies	£2.99
☐ The House that Sailed Away	Pat Hutchins	£2.99
☐ Rats!	Pat Hutchins	£2.99
☐ Burping Bertha	Michael Rosen	£2.50
☐ Who's Afraid of the Evil Eye?	Hazel Townson	£2.50
☐ Lenny and Jake Adventures	Hazel Townson	£2.99

PRICES AND OTHER DETAILS ARE LIABLE TO CHANGE

ARROW BOOKS, BOOKSERVICE BY POST, PO BOX 29, DOUGLAS, ISLE OF MAN, BRITISH ISLES

NAME..

ADDRESS ....

....

....

Please enclose a cheque or postal order made out to B.S.B.P. Ltd. for the amount due and allow the following for postage and packing:

U.K. CUSTOMERS: Please allow 75p per book to a maximum of £7.50

B.F.P.O. & EIRE: Please allow 75p per book to a maximum of £7.50

OVERSEAS CUSTOMERS: Please allow £1.00 per book.

While every effort is made to keep prices low it is sometimes necessary to increase cover prices at short notice. Arrow Books reserve the right to show new retail prices on covers which may differ from those previously advertised in the text or elsewhere.

BESTSELLING FICTION FROM RED FOX

☐	The Present Takers	Aidan Chambers	£2.99
☐	Battle for the Park	Colin Dann	£2.99
☐	Orson Cart Comes Apart	Steve Donald	£1.99
☐	The Last Vampire	Willis Hall	£2.99
☐	Harvey Angell	Diana Hendry	£2.99
☐	Emil and the Detectives	Erich Kästner	£2.99
☐	Krindlekrax	Philip Ridley	£2.99

PRICES AND OTHER DETAILS ARE LIABLE TO CHANGE

ARROW BOOKS, BOOKSERVICE BY POST, PO BOX 29, DOUGLAS, ISLE OF MAN, BRITISH ISLES

NAME ....

ADDRESS ....

....

....

Please enclose a cheque or postal order made out to B.S.B.P. Ltd. for the amount due and allow the following for postage and packing:

U.K. CUSTOMERS: Please allow 75p per book to a maximum of £7.50

B.F.P.O. & EIRE: Please allow 75p per book to a maximum of £7.50

OVERSEAS CUSTOMERS: Please allow £1.00 per book.

While every effort is made to keep prices low it is sometimes necessary to increase cover prices at short notice. Arrow Books reserve the right to show new retail prices on covers which may differ from those previously advertised in the text or elsewhere.

BESTSELLING FICTION FROM RED FOX

☐	The Story of Doctor Dolittle	Hugh Lofting	£3.99
☐	Amazon Adventure	Willard Price	£3.99
☐	Swallows and Amazons	Arthur Ransome	£3.99
☐	The Wolves of Willoughby Chase	Joan Aiken	£2.99
☐	Steps up the Chimney	William Corlett	£2.99
☐	The Snow-Walker's Son	Catherine Fisher	£2.99
☐	Redwall	Brian Jacques	£3.99
☐	Guilty!	Ruth Thomas	£2.99

PRICES AND OTHER DETAILS ARE LIABLE TO CHANGE

ARROW BOOKS, BOOKSERVICE BY POST, PO BOX 29, DOUGLAS, ISLE OF MAN, BRITISH ISLES

NAME ....

ADDRESS ....

....

....

Please enclose a cheque or postal order made out to B.S.B.P. Ltd. for the amount due and allow the following for postage and packing:

U.K. CUSTOMERS: Please allow 75p per book to a maximum of £7.50

B.F.P.O. & EIRE: Please allow 75p per book to a maximum of £7.50

OVERSEAS CUSTOMERS: Please allow £1.00 per book.

While every effort is made to keep prices low it is sometimes necessary to increase cover prices at short notice. Arrow Books reserve the right to show new retail prices on covers which may differ from those previously advertised in the text or elsewhere.

Other great reads ⌒ from **Red Fox**

Action-Packed Drama with Red Fox Fiction!

SIMPLE SIMON Yvonne Coppard

Simon isn't stupid – he's just not very good at practical things. So when Mum collapses, it's Cara, his younger sister who calls the ambulance and keeps a cool head. Simon plans to show what he can do too, in a crisis, but his plan goes frighteningly wrong . . .
ISBN 0 09 910531 4 £2.99

LOW TIDE William Mayne

Winner of the Guardian Children's Fiction Award.

The low tide at Jade Bay leaves fish on dry land and a wreck high on a rock. Is this the treasure ship the divers have been looking for? Three friends vow to find out – and find themselves swept away into adventure.
ISBN 0 09 918311 0 £3.50

THE INTRUDER John Rowe Townsend

It isn't often that you meet someone who claims to be you. But that's what happens to Arnold Haithwaite. The real Arnold has to confront the menacing intruder before he takes over his life completely.
ISBN 0 09 999260 4 £3.50

GUILTY Ruth Thomas

Everyone in Kate's class says that the local burglaries have been done by Desmond Locke's dad, because he's just come out of prison. Kate and Desmond think otherwise and set out to prove who really is *guilty*.
ISBN 0 09 918591 1 £2.99

Spinechilling stories to read at night

THE CONJUROR'S GAME Catherine Fisher

Alick has unwittingly set something unworldly afoot in Halcombe Great Wood.

ISBN 0 09 985960 2   £2.50

RAVENSGILL William Mayne

What is the dark secret that has held two families apart for so many years?

ISBN 0 09 975270 0   £2.99

EARTHFASTS William Mayne

The bizarre chain of events begins when David and Keith see someone march out of the ground . . .

ISBN 0 09 977600 6   £2.99

A LEGACY OF GHOSTS Colin Dann

Two boys go searching for old Mackie's hoard and find something else . . .

ISBN 0 09 986540 8   £2.99

TUNNEL TERROR

The Channel Tunnel is under threat and only Tom can save it . . .

ISBN 0 09 989030 5   £2.99

Other great reads from **Red Fox**

It's chocks away with Biggles and his chums by Captain W. E. Johns

That air ace and intrepid adventurer, Biggles, is guaranteed to offer thrill-packed adventure. Whether he's flying for his life in the skies above wartime France, or smashing a big crime ring in India, these stories make compulsive reading.

BIGGLES LEARNS TO FLY

In wartime France, it's a case of learn quickly or be killed . . .

ISBN 0 09 993820 0   £3.50

BIGGLES FLIES EAST

Biggles is sent on a dangerous spying mission to the Middle East where the least slip might cost him his life.

ISBN 0 09 993780 8   £3.50

BIGGLES & CO.

Transporting gold proves no easy job for Biggles.

ISBN 0 09 993800 6   £3.50

BIGGLES IN SPAIN

Caught in a bloody civil war, Biggles finds himself charged with getting valuable papers back to England.

ISBN 0 09 993810 3   £3.50

BIGGLES DEFIES THE SWASTIKA

Biggles is trapped in Norway by the invasion of the Nazis and in constant danger from his old enemy, Von Stalhein.

ISBN 0 09 993790 5   £3.50

BIGGLES IN THE ORIENT

Something is attacking the pilots making the wartime run from India to China – and it's up to Biggles to find out what.

ISBN 0 09 993830 8   £3.50

Other great reads from **Red Fox**

Share the magic of The Magician's House by William Corlett

There is magic in the air from the first moment the three Constant children, William, Mary and Alice arrive at their uncle's house in the Golden Valley. But it's when they meet the Magician, William Tyler, and hear of the Great Task he has for them that the adventures really begin.

THE STEPS UP THE CHIMNEY

Evil threatens Golden House in its hour of need – and the Magician's animals come to the children's aid – but travelling with a fox brings its own dangers.

ISBN 0 09 985370 1   £2.99

THE DOOR IN THE TREE

William, Mary and Alice find a cruel and vicious sport threatening the peace of Golden Valley on their return to this magical place.

ISBN 0 09 997390 1   £2.99

THE TUNNEL BEHIND THE WATERFALL

Evil creatures mass against the children as they attempt to master time travel.

ISBN 0 09 997910 1   £2.99

THE BRIDGE IN THE CLOUDS

With the Magician seriously ill, it's up to the three children to complete the Great Task alone.

ISBN 0 09 918301 9   £2.99